Chapter One

"Bet you can't."

"Bet I can."

"All right then." Henry Cashman stood up and polished his glasses on his sleeve. "Meet me here on the first day of the holidays, and we'll soon see who's made the most money. But remember the rules. You have to start from nothing. And you have to run the whole business yourself."

With that, he jammed his glasses on his nose, glinted dangerously and sauntered off to play "Zap The Aliens" with his friends from the Computer Club.

I leaned back against the park bench and groaned. How had I got myself into this stupid contest in the first place? If only I had ever learned to resist a challenge. But I hadn't. And I couldn't.

So when Henry had begun boasting about his amazing "Get-Rich-Quick" schemes I dived in without thinking —

"What makes you think you're so clever, Cashbags? I can make as much money as you any day. More, if you want to know. Much, much more."

So now here I was with one soft
mint, a couple of rubber bands and a
school dinner token in my pocket.
How on earth was I going to become a
pocket-money millionaire
before Easter?

"Dad," I asked in my sweetest voice
when he staggered home from work.
"If you wanted to make a fortune,
how would you
start?"

He looked at me wearily. He generally looked weary these days. He hadn't had the energy to visit his allotment for

months. "If I knew that," he said, "I wouldn't be running up and down stairs all day in an overcrowded shoe shop that's too cold in winter and too hot in summer and smells of damp socks. And you wouldn't need to ask." But he gave me fifty pence to go away and leave him in peace, so at least I'd made a start.

I tried Robbo next. My big brother.
He was always finding himself
Saturday jobs, so I reckoned he must
be a bit of an expert.

"Well," he said, chewing
thoughtfully on a banana toffee, "your
best bet would be a paper round, but
you're still too young. And in
any case, there aren't any
places free at the moment

because I've seen the waiting list and it's a mile long."

He took another toffee from the tube and studied it. "Maybe you could have a garage sale? Clear out your cupboards. Your room's full of useless junk."

That was the trouble. After I'd
sorted everything into heaps, the only
stuff I could bear to sell was either
broken or battered, or had never
worked in the first place.

"No one's going to buy this old
rubbish," I grumbled. So I left it
on the bedroom floor and
went to consult
Celia.

Chapter Two

Celia was Robbo's girlfriend. Still is. Though what she sees in my brother I'll never know. Anyway, she used to pop round most evenings to help him with his homework, and what she didn't know about facts and figures wasn't worth knowing.

"What you have to do," she said, flicking her long black braids over her shoulders, "is study the market. Ask questions. What do your friends need? What can they afford to pay? And what can you offer them? Simple!"

Simple, I thought. Oh yes? And I trailed off to try Mum. She was in the kitchen prodding at a pot of brown leaves. She hates gardening. That's why we live in a flat. I grabbed a bent fork and took over.

"What do people want?" I asked, rummaging through the roots.

"More money," said Mum. "Don't make a mess, dear."

I sighed and tried again. "But what do they want to buy? I mean, what sort of shops are always busy?"

Mum dunked her hands in a bowl of soapy water. "Shoe shops. Chemists. Hairdressers. Anywhere that sells food. Why?"

I didn't answer. The whole thing was hopeless. I couldn't make shoes.

I couldn't cure diseases. I couldn't cut hair. Well, not without causing a riot, anyway. And Miss Fanshaw reckoned I was the worst cook she'd ever taught. Even my jellies could loosen your teeth.

"I'll never get rich at this rate," I muttered, attacking the dry dirt with a spoon. "The only thing I'm really good at is digging holes."

But the following morning a perfect idea arrived from a totally unexpected direction. Miss Fanshaw had asked us to write a story about our favourite pets, and one by one we all read out

our descriptions. With the single exception of Joey Reece, who had invented a tame dinosaur that ate chocolate buttons, everyone seemed to have said the same thing.

"I had a big dog called Jupiter. He could balance a biscuit on his nose and he liked playing with my dad's slippers. And then he died."

"My cat was grey so her name was Smoky. She was always sleeping on my mum's best jumpers and she used to climb up the curtains. But she got run over and she died."

"Our hamster could escape from anything. Once he wriggled out of his cage and ate my sister's homework. He even climbed the stairs and hid under my bed. But one day when we woke up he was dead."

21

It was the gloomiest collection of stories ever written, but Miss Fanshaw didn't seem to notice. "Very good," she said, dishing out sticky stars in all directions. "Lovely drawings. Well done everyone."

But I was on the edge of my seat. At last I knew what my business was going to be.

Chapter Three

That evening I shoved Robbo out of the way and plonked myself next to Celia. "Funerals for small pets," I whispered. "Give your fluffy friends a fond farewell. How do I start?"

"I'll print some adverts for you on my word processor," she said. "But have you made proper plans? I mean, what are you going to do with all those poor little bodies?"

"All sorted," I said proudly. "I've offered to dig the allotment for Dad. It's the ideal spot. Dark and quiet and gloomy. And he's going to pay me with empty shoe boxes."

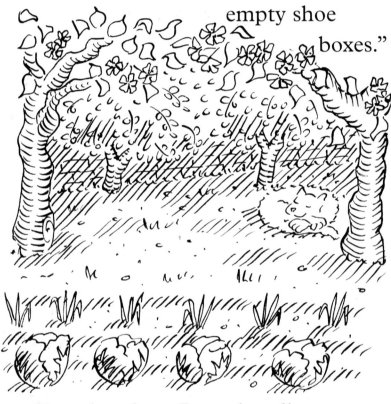

Two days later I was handing out leaflets to every pet owner in the school. "Frankie's Furry Funerals", they announced. "Have you lost a loved one? Want to give your pets a superior send-off? Then contact Francesca in Class M. (PS All animals must be small enough to fit inside a shoe box.)"

I thought it sounded too corny. All that "lost-a-loved-one" stuff. But Celia said it would strike a chord, so I slapped black paint on the boxes and crossed my fingers.

After the first week, I must admit I was beginning to despair. The only response so far was from a spindly boy in Year 6 who wanted me to bury his stick insect. It was so tiny it fitted inside

a matchbox, and
the whole thing
was over in
fifteen seconds.

After all, what
can you say about a stick insect?
"We'll all miss you very much. The
way you used to wiggle your front legs.
The great games
of Hide and Seek
you used to play."

I covered the pitiful hole quickly and stuck a seed label in the dirt. It just said "No. 1", as the insect hadn't been given a name. I charged its owner twenty pence, which seemed a bit over the top but he didn't complain. He skipped away looking really pleased, so at least I had

one satisfied customer. Or two, if you counted the stick insect.

Then, out of nowhere, business improved. Maybe the stick insect's owner had recommended me. I don't know, but in three days I had four customers. Granted, two of them were sisters, but they were prepared to pay for a double ceremony so that was all right.

And very moving it was, too. They
had won a pair of goldfish at the fair,
and their prizes had died overnight in
a jam jar of tap water. So Flipper and
Jaws were buried together in a circular
grave, which we decorated with
coloured gravel and a plastic
shipwreck.

Everyone was in tears, and I was still blowing my nose when Suzy Lee arrived with her gerbil. "I've got a poem to read out," she lisped. "And a real wreath. And I want a cross."

So I fixed two lolly sticks together while she recited:

"O Lulu Lee, I'm feeling ill,
'Cos you're not here, my best gerbil."

"Very nice," I said. "I'm sure she'll appreciate that."

"Don't be silly," snapped Suzy. "Lulu's a boy. And he's dead."

So I just smoothed the earth into a tidy heap and planted the ring of daisies where I was told. I think Suzy was satisfied, but it was Rover Johnson's funeral that really made my reputation.

Chapter Four

Rover was a budgie. One sunny day he had squawked, "Rover wants a Smartie", kicked his wobbly man and collapsed. His owner was a huge boy called Lewis, with muscles like an orang-utan and a voice to match.

"He was my mate," growled Lewis.
"You treat him right and I'll treat you
right. Right?"

"Right," I twittered. I lowered the
box into its hole, cleared my throat
and rambled on about the sunshine
and the rain and the spring flowers,
and Rover's little feathered spirit
soaring away on a rainbow of freedom.
Honestly, I was so scared I didn't
know what I was
saying.

I patted the mound into shape, stuck a lump of cuttlefish in the top and waited for Lewis to thump me with the shovel.

When I finally turned round his face was all puffy. He bunged several coins into my hand and lurched away muttering, "Thank you" in a thin, bird-like croak.

After that, the orders poured in. As the weeks rolled by, I was sure I had made enough money to buy Celia an Easter egg and still win my bet.

37

Frankie's Famous Funerals were bound to beat Henry's boring old schemes, weren't they? His carwashing service wasn't exactly original, and his home-made popcorn was usually a bit black and chewy. I could hardly wait to see the look on Cashbag's face when I showed him my fortune.

Then just before the
end of term
something took my
mind off money-
making. Julia Lacey, a
girl in our class, fell ill. She wasn't a
special friend, but she had always been
there, ever since our first day. And
now we could tell from the careful
quietness of Miss Fanshaw's voice that
there was something seriously wrong.

She explained to us about operations and transplants and the search for a cure, while we sat staring at our thumbs and wondering what we could do to help. Someone put a collection box on the bookcase

by the door, and every evening we pushed past it on our way home. I couldn't get Julia Lacey out of my head. I wanted to see her back in her old seat. I wanted to hear her giggle again.

"Have a wonderful holiday, children," Miss Fanshaw said as the final bell rang. "And let's hope I have some good news for you all after Easter."

I was the last one out of the classroom for once. I was thinking about my meeting with Cashbags tomorrow. The big show-down. Henry's Last Stand.

Chapter Five

A clown stood outside the park gates next morning. Behind her red nose she looked suspiciously like Miss Fanshaw, and she was shaking a large plastic bucket with Julia's picture stuck on the front. I hung around for a while, wishing my money-belt didn't feel so uncomfortable. Then I hurried away to reach the bench by the swings.

"So how much did you make?" demanded Henry.

I opened my hand to reveal a single silver coin. "Actually there was a bit more than that," I began miserably. "But it sort of disappeared. How much did you make?" And I forced myself to look him in the eyes.

He was grinning, of course. Then he
pushed a single silver coin towards me.
"Actually," he said, "I put all the rest
in the bucket too."

And it's a funny thing, but we've been friends ever since. In fact, I quite enjoy Henry's chewy popcorn now. I still do the occasional funeral if I'm asked, and everyone says how well-dug the allotment looks these days.

Only Dad seems slightly puzzled.
He's never quite worked out what it is
I'm supposed to be planting.

S/442001-J.

46